For Max, Tilly and
Bobbi Dazzler

xxx

The Snowman Strikes Back © 2016 by Allan Plenderleith
For more books by Allan visit allanplenderleith.com

First published in 2016
by
Ravette Publishing Limited
PO Box 876, Horsham, West Sussex RH12 9GH

ISBN: 978-1-84161-393-2
Printed and bound in India by Replika Press Pvt. Ltd.

The Snowman Strikes Back

by Allan Plenderleith

RAVETTE PUBLISHING

It's not easy being a snowman.

Especially when you've been made by this boy...
Ernest Green-Bogle, the meanest kid in town!

Every year when snow has fallen
Ernest runs outside and makes me.

But he doesn't do it for fun, oh no.

He does it so he can be EVIL!

He makes me look like this.

And this.

And even this.

He likes to do this to me.

And this.

And even this.

He turned me into a snow clown.
Not funny.

And a snow cone!

No it's not much fun being
Ernest Green-Bogle's snowman.

But one day everything changed.

It was four o'clock, and Ernest
came home from school as usual,
but he wasn't alone.

A big boy was with him.

Ernest has made a new friend, I thought.
But as they came nearer I heard the boy say:

"And you better not tell
anyone where you got that
black eye or I'll need to eat your
packed lunch again tomorrow!"

I couldn't believe it!
Ernest was being bullied.

He wasn't the meanest kid
in town after all.

The big kid stomped off and
a sad Ernest sat down
on the ground beside me and cried.

"There there, don't worry Ernest," I said.

"Aargh!" screamed Ernest and he jumped up.
"Wh...who...ss...said that?"

"It's me, your snowman," I replied.

I explained to Ernest that
all snowmen and snowladies are alive,
we're just not supposed to talk.

One of the rules you see.

When he calmed down
I asked about his black eye.
But Ernest didn't want to
talk about it and ran inside.

The next day, Ernest walked past me
on the way to school but didn't say anything.

He looked at me strangely,
perhaps he thought he had imagined
talking to his snowman.

But later that day, Ernest came home
with the big boy again.
This time with another black eye.

"This time keep your mouth shut about
me or I'll shut it for you!" said the bully.

The big boy left, laughing, and Ernest sat down
beside me in tears once again.

"You know, you don't have to
put up with that," I said.

"What do you know about being bullied?"
said Ernest. "You're just a stupid snowman."

I told him that every year
a little boy has been horrid to me
and that I didn't like it at all.

Ernest realised that
the little boy was him.

"I have an idea how we can
stop this big bully Ernest,
but you're going to have to help me."

"Oh, and we're going to need more snow..."

That night, the big bully slept
in his bed, his greedy tummy full from all
the packed lunches he had stolen from
Ernest and lots of other little girls and boys.

Suddenly there was a tap at the window.
The bully awoke, frightened.

Tap tap tap. What could it be?

He crept out of bed and
nervously approached the window.

But there was nothing there
but icy darkness. Until...

The bully screamed and
hid under his duvet quivering.

Ernest and I had done it!
That had shown the big bully.

But there was one more thing left to do.

The next morning the big bully
awoke to the sound of a commotion outside.

Outside, all the town had gathered
round the bully's house to see
the most amazing thing.

Ernest was never bullied again,
and was always a wonderful friend.

So remember to look out
for me when it snows.

I'm the one with the biggest smile.

The End

Note from the author

Bullying can happen to anyone at any age. Being bullied at school, home or online might involve someone pushing you, hitting you, teasing you, talking about you or calling you names. Nobody has the right to hurt you or make you feel bad. You don't have to deal with things alone.

You can get support by asking an adult for help or by visiting

childline.org.uk

Allan
x

More Christmas books by Allan Plenderleith:

The Christmas Carrot
Everyone wants a piece of me!
by Allan Plenderleith

The Bonkers Banana
by Allan Plenderleith

The Tiny Tree
Can I be your Christmas tree?...
by Allan Plenderleith

The Silly Satsuma
What can a silly satsuma do?
by Allan Plenderleith

The Smelly Sprout
Why does nobody like me?
by Allan Plenderleith

Complete your collection!

allanplenderleith.com